Panda Purim

by Jennifer Tzivia MacLeod

Panda Purim © 5775 Jennifer Tzivia MacLeod

ISBN-13: 978-1502332288
ISBN-10: 1502332280

Not everybody
looks forward to Purim.

Pandas, for instance.
It's tough for them to get in the mood.

Pandas are almost too mellow
for Purim.

They'd really rather
just sit around.

He never knows
what to dress up as.

No matter what he picks, everybody
always guesses he's a panda.

And what can he send his
friends and family for
mishloach manot when all
they want to eat is bamboo?

Not that there's anything wrong with bamboo.

Sure, Purim is a chance
to have fun with his friends.

But how can anybody expect him
to sit still through the whole
megillah reading?

It's not his fault he sometimes makes noise at the wrong time.

He really thought he heard them say, "Haman."

There's not a single panda
in the story of Purim.

Then again, Hashem's name
isn't in there either.

Not everybody
looks forward to Purim…

And it's true that most days,
he'd really rather stay home.

But even though getting ready can sometimes make him cranky…

...In the end,
he's really glad it's here.

Chag Sameach!

חַג שָׂמֵחַ!

Bonus:

How to fold your very own Origami Pandas:

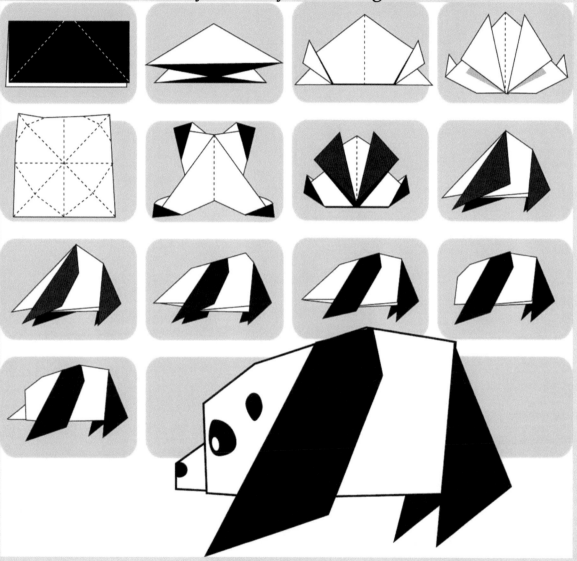

Hint: Use black and white paper, of course, for the most panda-looking panda. Or go wild and use any color you want!

The Jewish Nature Series:

Penguin Rosh Hashanah

Caterpillar Yom Kippur

Turtle Sukkot

Owl Hanukkah

Panda Purim

Otter Passover

Elephant Tisha b'Av

Discover them all at:
http://tinyurl.com/JewishNature

About the Author:

Jennifer Tzivia MacLeod is a proud mother of four (two big and two little), who lives in northern Israel.   A freelance writer for magazines and newspapers, she also loves writing stories for her kids and their friends.

Can you help me out?

As an independent writer, I don't have a big company promoting my books. I count on readers like you to leave feedback for others so I can keep on writing. If you and your kids enjoyed this book, please take a minute, head over to Amazon, and let others know.

Thanks! ☺

Made in the USA
Coppell, TX
21 February 2021